ADVENTURE ANNIE
Goes To
Kindergarten

by
Toni Buzzeo

illustrated by
Amy Wummer

DIAL BOOKS FOR YOUNG READERS
an imprint of Penguin Group (USA) Inc.

To all of the fabulous kindergarten teachers
I've taught with—and especially Todd
—T.B.

To the dedicated, hardworking teachers we know and love—gold stars to all!
—A.W.

DIAL BOOKS FOR YOUNG READERS
A division of Penguin Young Readers Group
Published by The Penguin Group
Penguin Group (USA) Inc., 375 Hudson Street, New York, NY 10014, U.S.A.
Penguin Group (Canada), 90 Eglinton Avenue East, Suite 700, Toronto, Ontario, Canada M4P 2Y3
(a division of Pearson Penguin Canada Inc.)
Penguin Books Ltd, 80 Strand, London WC2R 0RL, England
Penguin Ireland, 25 St. Stephen's Green, Dublin 2, Ireland (a division of Penguin Books Ltd)
Penguin Group (Australia), 250 Camberwell Road, Camberwell, Victoria 3124, Australia
(a division of Pearson Australia Group Pty Ltd)
Penguin Books India Pvt Ltd, 11 Community Centre, Panchsheel Park, New Delhi - 110 017, India
Penguin Group (NZ), 67 Apollo Drive, Rosedale, North Shore 0632, New Zealand
(a division of Pearson New Zealand Ltd)
Penguin Books (South Africa) (Pty) Ltd, 24 Sturdee Avenue, Rosebank, Johannesburg 2196, South Africa
Penguin Books Ltd, Registered Offices: 80 Strand, London WC2R 0RL, England
Designed by Jasmin Rubero
Text set in ITC Esprit
Manufactured in China on acid-free paper

1 3 5 7 9 10 8 6 4 2

Library of Congress Cataloging-in-Publication Data
Buzzeo, Toni.
Adventure Annie goes to kindergarten / by Toni Buzzeo ; illustrated by Amy Wummer.
p.   cm.
Summary: Even though there are rules to follow, a little girl who
loves adventure has an exciting first day of kindergarten.
ISBN 978-0-8037-3358-9 (hardcover)
[1. First day of school—Fiction. 2. Kindergarten—Fiction. 3. Schools—Fiction.
4. Adventure and adventurers—Fiction.] I. Wummer,
Amy, ill. II. Title.
PZ7.B9832Ac 2010
[E]—dc22
2009023818

The illustrations were prepared using pencil and
watercolor on Strathmore Bristol paper.

"Rise and shine, Adventure Annie,"
Mommy sings at my door.

I hop to my calendar.

At last!

Adventure Annie kindergarten day.

"Will I have a wild animal
  zoo adventure?"
"Maybe not today,"
  says Mommy.

"Will I have a high-flying
  circus adventure?"
"Maybe *after* school,"
  says Mommy.

"What about a daring search-and-find rescue adventure?"
"Maybe on the weekend,"
says Mommy.

I throw my arms out wide.

"Well then, what adventure *will* I have at kindergarten?"

"Sometimes," Mommy says,
"kindergarten is its own adventure."
  I give her the Adventure Annie thumbs-up.

I squizzle back to my room
and tuck my zookeeper hat,
my high wire slippers,
and my walkie-talkies into my
backpack—
just in case.

"Let's go!" I sing.

We hop to it.

I push through the tall glass doors
of Pioneer Elementary School.

I kiss Mommy good-bye,

then knock-knock-knock
on the kindergarten door.
I burst inside.

"Adventure Annie is here!" I shout.

A tall man rushes over to shake my hand.

"Hello," he says.

"I'm Mr. Todd. Who are you?"

I point to the A on my shirt.

He glances at a clipboard.
"Annie Grace?"

I nod my head and swirl my cape.
"Adventure Annie."

Mr. Todd taps a
hook marked
Annie
but I wrap myself up tight.

"I need my cape."
"Well then," he says, "let's find your seat."

I follow Mr. Todd straight to a table
that matches my red cape perfectly.
I slip into a chair between two other kids.

"I'm Adventure Annie.
Who are you?"
"José," the boy says.
"And that's Louise."

Louise just ducks her head.

On the circle rug, Mr. Todd explains our
Kindergarten Gold Star Rules.

Gold Star Rules
1. Respect our classroom and everything in it.
2. Make good decisions.
3. Use your inside voices.
4. Be kind and helpful to others.

"But what about adventures?" I ask.
"You're right, Annie," Mr. Todd says.
"The most important rule of all is
'Enjoy your kindergarten adventure!'"

Then he taps his shiny gold star.

"Each day, I will choose my **Gold Star Deputy**."

I wave my hand in big circles. **"Here I am!"**

Mr. Todd looks at me.

"We don't know who it will be quite yet, Annie."

"Does it depend on our kindergarten adventures?" I ask.

He tilts his head to the side.

"Yes, your adventures with the Gold Star Rules."

During morning snack at the red table,
I wear my zookeeper hat.

I pop wild animal fruit snacks into my mouth.
"How about a wild animal zoo adventure?"
Louise and José just blink.

Behind José's chair, I spot
three squeaky hamsters in a cage.
What those squeakers need
is a natural habitat exhibit.

Luckily, the art supplies are ready for me.

Clap-clap.
Clap
clap
clap.

The room is quiet.
Mr. Todd squats next to me
and looks at the cage.
"Oh dear," he says.

"Remember the Gold Star Rule, Annie?
Take good care of our classroom
and everything in it."
"Oopsie." I hand him
the paintbrush.
"Back to your seat, please,"
he says.

At the red table,
   I slide into my high wire slippers.

"How about a high-flying circus adventure?"
   But Louise and José just stare.
   Am I the only one looking for Gold Star adventures?

The jungle gym sparkles in the sun
just outside the window.
While Mr. Todd washes off the hamster cage,
I slip out the courtyard door
and fly onto the empty climber.

Suddenly, I see Mr. Todd below me.

"Remember the
Gold Star Rule,
Annie?

"Make good decisions."
He points me back inside.

All during story circle

and math centers

and lunch,

I watch for new adventure opportunities.
I imagine that gold star pinned under my chin.

"Afternoon snack time!" Mr. Todd calls.
"I need two helpers to fetch milk.
Who remembers where the cafeteria is?"
I wave in big circles,
but Mr. Todd calls on Louise and José.

We wait for the milk.

And wait.

And wait.

Finally, Mr. Todd says, "I need a helper to fetch the milk fetchers. They must be lost."

This time my waving works.

"Annie, why don't you go? But remember the Gold Star Rule. Use your inside voice."

I grab my walkie-talkies
and teach Mr. Todd
how they work.

Then I ziggle
and zaggle

through the **whole** school.

"Not in the library," I whisper to Mr. Todd.

"Not in the cafeteria.

"Not in the
bathrooms, either.

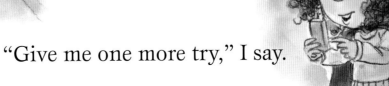

"Give me one more try," I say.

I peek in at a door marked
PRINCIPAL.
　　Right there,
behind a wagon full of milk,
I spot the worried faces of
　　Louise and José.

I knock-knock-knock
and burst inside.
In my loudest whisper I say,

"Adventure Annie to the rescue!"

A short lady comes to meet me.

"Wonderful," she says.

"We were just about to walk down to kindergarten."

I lead Louise, José, and the milk wagon down the hall.

"We're on our way,"
    I whisper into my walkie-talkie.

"**Way to go,
Adventure Annie!**"
    says Mr. Todd.

We don't stop for a single adventure
on our way back to kindergarten.

At our closing circle,
Mr. Todd calls, "Annie Grace."

"Adventure Annie,"
I remind him.
Then he pins the gold star right beneath
my chin after all.

Adventure Annie,

Gold Star Deputy, to the rescue!